愛的燈塔
Love's Lighthouse

星子安娜雙語詩選

Anna Yin 著

謹以此書獻給在路上的人們，
讓愛的燈塔照亮你，也照亮我。

the long journey

with my whole heart

I want to love you back

作者介紹

　　星子安娜（Anna Yin）加拿大密西沙加市第一屆桂冠詩人，生於中國湖南，92年南京大學電腦系畢業，99年移民加拿大。安娜榮獲2005年安大略省詩人協會詩歌獎，2010／2014密市文學獎，2013加拿大中國專業人士協會的專業成就獎以及2016／2017年西切斯特大學詩歌大會獎學金和安大略省藝術文學項目獎等。安娜中英文詩歌在中國日報，紐約時報，世界日報，加拿大文學評論，世界詩歌等刊物發表，著有四本英文詩集，獲得加拿大國家桂冠詩人和總督文學獲獎詩人以及主流媒體的好評。2011年和2012年安娜被選入75位候選人競選最佳25名加拿大移民獎，並連續兩次當選為加拿大詩人聯盟全國理事和安省代表。安娜作品也被加拿大國家詩歌月和全國公交巡展詩歌選用，安娜多次在國際詩歌節表演和講授詩歌，並擔任詩歌評委和策劃人。

安娜網站：www.annapoetry.com

About the author

Anna Yin was Mississauga's Inaugural Poet Laureate. She was born in Hunan, China, graduated from Nanjing University in 1992 and emigrated to Canada in 1999. Anna has authored six poetry books and won awards including the 2005 Ted Plantos Memorial Award, 2010/2014 MARTYs, 2013 Professional Achievement Award from CPAC, 2016/2017 scholarships from West Chester University Poetry Conference and three grants from Ontario Arts Council etc. Her poems in English & Chinese and ten translations by her were in a Canadian Studies textbook used by Humber College. With poems published in ARC Poetry, New York Times, CBC, World Journal, Room, Cha, China Daily etc. Anna has been interviewed by CBC Radio, Rogers TV, CCTV and TalentVisionTV, The Toronto Star etc. She was a finalist for Canada's Top 25 Canadian

Immigrants Award in 2011 and in 2012. She served as Ontario representative for the League of Canadian Poets from 2013 to 2016. Her poem "Still Life" was displayed on 700 buses across Canada for the Poetry In Transit project and "My Accent" was read at the 2014 Chinese New Year Celebration at Parliament Hill, Ottawa. Her readings and Poetry Alive workshops were featured at International Poetry Festivals and she has served on renowned poetry book awards juries in Canada.

website: www.annapoetry.com

東評西說

　　星子的詩歌充實而氣韻自如、清新淡雅而又柔巧乾淨，也有暗示和張力，典型的在回憶中尋找美麗的女性詩歌。星子是湖南人，但她的詩歌裡沒有屈原詩歌濃重的悲劇色彩，以及「楚雖三戶，亡秦必楚也」的壯烈，這是今天一代人的幸福使然。但是，在她的詩歌裡，還是可以感受到湘楚文化裡決絕淒美的回聲，同時，又蘊涵和散發著對美好生命的熱烈。在當今這個浮躁的白晝時代，詩歌正如清夜的星子。

　　　　　　　　　　——川沙（加拿大華語詩人協會會長）

　　星子的詩作，精巧、優美、空靈、清新，把中國古典詩歌的品質帶到流暢、鮮明的英語裡。她以感人和豐富的想像力，富有現代感的經驗和意識，展示了真正的跨國的聲音和情感，以及全球的人文觀和文化素養。

　　　　　　　　　　——布萊思・馬斯特（多倫多，詩人，編輯）

星子用細膩、清麗、質樸和有張力的語言之筆，為我們
創造了一個充滿愛，充滿美，充滿寧靜和自然的精神世界。

——何均（中國四川，詩人，小說家）

星子安娜長期在《創世紀》發表詩作，廣受喜愛和肯
定。她不但中文詩寫得好，英文詩更屢獲大獎。除了中英
詩創作，她亦精於翻譯，作為詩人她對文字的敏銳度和詩意
涵的拿捏有超乎尋常表現，《愛的燈塔》既是心靈之旅，也
是中西文化融合的體驗，值得推薦。

——辛牧（台灣《創世紀詩雜誌》總編輯）

星子的作品中，古典情懷與現代精神、詩歌技巧與人
性本真、異國情調與故土牽掛交織在一起，向我們訴說著一
個疏離、憂傷、沉思和慰藉的詩歌語境。生活裡的她率真開
朗，美麗而又明媚。人與詩不尋常的分裂與一致也許正是現
實與夢境的縮影以及內心深處的寫照。

——阿九（溫哥華，詩人，

近期譯著《菲力浦·拉金詩全集》）

從我早年譯介歐美現代詩，到用漢語寫詩，用英語翻
譯，再到後來用漢英雙語寫詩的經驗，我能深深感受到星子
在雙語詩所展示的兩種不同文化和不同語言的體驗與結合。
每首雙語詩，無論是從漢語或英語開始，都是一種再創作，

而不是單純的互譯，由此帶給讀者的詩意與樂趣，遠勝過單
語詩。

——非馬（美國伊利諾州詩人協會前任會長）

這種對生命的體驗由星子娓娓道來的時候，就像一股清
流，自然而透徹地拂拭著每個聽者心頭躁動的浮塵。

——明報加東版

與其說星子的雙語詩能遊刃有餘於中西文壇，是她才華
橫溢的必然，不如說是人生的歷練豐盈她的遼闊。她以詩裡
行間的綺麗和深思與時間抗衡，在同現實的和解中跳出現實
的框架，用詩照亮自己也照亮他人。

——姚園（美國《常青藤》詩刊主編）

星子的詩讓我想到智利詩人米斯特拉爾和義大利的黃昏
隱逸派，而且也想到中國的宋朝詩。星子有平常人的心態，
又經過西方自由博愛的思想洗禮，她的詩樸素親切，優美婉
約，純淨自然富有妙趣。

——溫東華（中國湖北，詩人、評論家）

作為一個成熟的詩人，星子總是淡定地把自己的心思娓
娓道來，一股清新，一抹黛色，總是那麼宜人。從對自然物
景的描寫，到對人的情感敘述，以及自己對人生的追求，都

是那麼淡定著傾注於語言中，簡單而不淺薄，由此把自己定格在從容不迫的格調上，讓自己充實而厚重，洗盡鉛華呈素姿。

——蔡利華（中國重慶，詩人，作家）

與普通中英文簡單互譯的詩集不同，這本詩集的獨特之處是針對同一內容的中英文的獨立創作。作者是成熟的漢語詩人，同時在英語詩人中享有盛譽。可以說這本詩集只有作者，沒有譯者。中文詩和英文詩各存異趣，交相輝映，各自承載了兩種文字的美感。這為中英比較文學提供了一個範例。

——曉鳴（北美中西文化交流協會會長）

星子一直在異國以詩歌的寧靜打量著光怪陸離、變化莫測的世界，並且渴望用詩歌給身體和靈魂找一個合適存在的位置。星子以詩歌來表述生命的行走狀態，是一種在詩意中行走，是海德格爾所說的美，這種美是在星子詩意的棲居裡呈現。

——鐘磊（中國長春，詩人、評論家）

（依照筆畫排列）

Reviews from the West

Anna Yin's poems give us beauty in all its delicacy and its strength—a full glowing presence that sometimes, mysteriously, is just a fleeting hint, a dance of shadows. The poet of *Love's Lighthouse* resolutely "wants to add more windows" to her house of poetry, not to increase its price, "but just because you live there". She realizes that her "days are full / even tears are golden". I love the beauty of her rhythms and the creativity of her phrasing wedded to an agile mind moving like a butterfly in a flower garden of thought: "Into a forest / you follow a sound. / The child you are, / searches for seeds of passion fruit; / instead, leaves of autumn fall over you..." But for a poet such as Yin, a creative and exploratory spirit, autumn cannot be just a symbol of sadness: the leaves' "rich colors / make a maze of wonderland." This is an original poet following her intuition ever deeper into the secrets of emotion and reality.

—A. F. Moritz, 6th Toronto Poet Laureate,
2009 Griffin Poetry Prize Winner

Beautiful verses and powerful images touched many readers.

—Alan Neal, host, CBC Radio

In Yin's poems, concrete things also seem to lift off their pages. Yin transforms—even transfigures—them with her imagination, through descriptions of dreams and through allusions to myths and cultural sayings...

—Doyali Islam, editor of ARC Poetry

An authentic, direct tone brings the author's native Chinese voice to these poems, which are charming and fresh at their best.

—Elena Wolff, poet and editor

Yin is endlessly perspicacious, endlessly compelling... She brings to Canadian poetry a sense of classicism and aestheticism and minimalism, all nicely mixed up with sensuality.

—George Elliott Clarke, 7th Parliamentary
Poet Laureate of Canada

Anna Yin's delicate, sensitive and haunting poetry will sweep you off your feet, carry you to exciting, exotic places and land you right in your own backyard. From her carefully crafted Haiku, to her sorrowful, melodic, sweet verses, you will not be able to put her work down, nor will you be able to read those beautiful poems only once. You will want to read them over and over again.

—I.B. Iskov, editor and founder
of the Ontario Poetry Society

It is a beautiful book, crafted by a beautiful poet. You have a great tell-tale line. It is "You outlive." Beautiful, beautiful.

—John Robert Colombo, writer

To read the poetry of Anna Yin is to court the landscape of ecstasy…It is a way to「be」, to watch nature, a vase of flowers dying with the same wonder one regards the Milky Way on a clear and endless summer night…This is the deep listening that brings to mind poets like Rainer Maria Rilke or Lee Young-Li, using nature as a guide toward stillness. Anna Yin's stillness is one where time is not part of its alchemy. There is a classic, masterful touch, an underlying Taoist's inscription…

—Lois P. Jones, poet, host on KPFK's Poets Café and editor of Kyoto Journal.

The blending of East and West adds a fascinating dimension to her oeuvre. Her unique voice represents a new direction in contemporary Canadian literature.

—Paul Hartal, painter and poet

Yin has a unique way of weaving together on the loom of her poetic vision the layered wealth of Chinese thought and culture with the probing demands of Canadian and American poetic visionaries--rare is such a combination and genius. But, there is yet a fuller synthesis. Poets and painters are called forth, in an even more cosmopolitan manner, to inform and shape the literary life of Anna Yin: Dante, Akhmatova, Van Gogh, Burns, Borges, Basho and Yeats step forward on the stage of Anna's poetic oeuvre and speak, suggestively and wisely, of deeper and more demanding truths.

—Ron Dart, author and professor

Anna Yin is a fine writer with a true feel for the power of nature and the healing strength of wilderness.

—Roy MacGregor, writer and historian

Not all poets have the talent for honing in on just the right word, but Yin possesses that rare gift.

—Sandy Millar, Mississauga News

"Raspberries" is a concise exploration of a moment; a modern interpretation of the kind of classical Chinese poems in which a specific scene, thought or feeling is condensed and captured in the most economic way, yet still allows for a number of interpretations.

—Tammy Ho, Cha: An Asian Literary Journal

序言

理查德・格林

（曉鳴翻譯）

「你漫步在門口，

呼吸著兩種語言」

近年來，星子安娜正成為加拿大詩壇一位引人注目的詩人，她的成就值得更廣為人知。她已經出版了六本詩集，並當選密西沙加的首位桂冠詩人。她參加過很多文化活動和公益事業。她的很多詩出現在一系列的出版物當中。她還積極參與詩歌的中英文互譯。

《愛的燈塔》是一部重要並抱負不凡的中英文雙語詩集。我只能閱讀一種語言，因此羨慕那些能欣賞兩種語言的讀者。

幾年前我寫到，星子的詩與二十世紀初的意象派有共通之處。她用精煉的文字，水晶般的意象，表達出強烈的情感和深刻的含義。她往往用簡潔明瞭的直接陳述去描繪詩中人物的感受，並主要依賴客體之間的優雅並置去激發讀者的興趣。她的詩歌往往帶有神祕感，就像一個夢無縫地潛入另一個夢，無需停頓去相互實證。

這本詩集中我最喜歡的是〈陌〉，它是這樣開頭的：

　　通往她房間的門關上；
　　那裡有著整個世界。

這首詩連續描述了一位男子的三次拜訪。第一次，他留下一張紙條，她將其折疊成了仙鶴。然後他把草帽留在門口，而在房間裡，一朵玫瑰散落了花瓣，她將花瓣張貼在鏡子上。最後，他帶來一條長絲巾，蒙著雙眼，他們一起進入房間。我不知道這個敘事中的每個元素意味著什麼──但我能感覺到戀人之間的交談以神祕的方式在親密行為中結束。

這本詩集中的許多詩都是以這種方式展開的──輕靈純樸，有時是通過夢幻般的情境，在讀者中引起由衷的反應。

這本詩集充滿了召喚和聯想的小奇蹟。星子安娜引起了我們的密切關注。《愛的燈塔》是一本非常精彩的書。

注：

　　理查德・格林，多倫多大學英語教授，是四本詩集的作者，同時也是國際知名的伊蒂絲希特維爾的傳記的作者。他的《搏擊指南針》獲得2010年加拿大總督文學詩歌獎。

　　曉鳴，中國四川人，曾任北美中西文化交流協會會長。1981年開始發表詩歌，小說和散文。

Preface

"Around the doorway, you wander,
breathe in two languages."

In the past few years, Anna Yin has become a considerable figure in Canadian poetry, though perhaps not as widely known as she ought to be. She has published six books of poems and served as Mississauga's inaugural poet laureate. She has participated in many cultural festivals and public events, and individual poems of hers have appeared in an array of publications. She has also become an active translator of poetry.

Love's Lighthouse is an important and ambitious collection, for here she gives us her poems in both Chinese and English. As one who can only read the English versions, I must admit to envy those who can read both.

Some years ago, I wrote that Anna Yin's poetry has

much in common with the Imagists of the early twentieth century. She writes a pared down verse, which relies on crystalline images to communicate powerful emotion. She makes just a few direct statements about what her persona is feeling, relying instead on the elegant juxtaposition of one object and another to stir the reader.

Often her poems are enigmatic, just as in dreams one possibility emerges out of another without pausing to justify itself.

Among my favorite compositions in this book is "The Path" – it begins:

> The door to her room is closed;
> there is a whole world there.

The poem goes on to describe three visits from a man. The first time, he brings a note which the woman folds into a paper crane. Then he leaves his hat at the door, while inside the room a rose loses its petals, which are then attached to a mirror. Finally, he brings a long scarf and, both blindfolded, they go into the room together. I don't know what each element in this narrative *means*–but I can sense a conversation of lovers that ends in mystery and intimacy.

Many poems in this collection work just in this manner–
simple, sometimes dreamlike, situations evoke in the reader
a heartfelt response.

This book is full of small miracles of evocation and
association. Anna Yin has earned our close attention. *Love's
Lighthouse* is a wonderful book.

Richard Greene

Professor of English, University of Toronto

*攝影、設計｜管濤

CONTENTS

故鄉的風 Winds from Hometown

在路上

On the Journey

日子是飽滿的
甚至眼淚　都金燦燦的

翻過去的書頁
每一行都是光亮
來自愛的燈塔

my days are full
even tears are golden

all turned pages
each line is glowing
from love's lighthouse

* 攝影｜時影

夢

隨著一種聲音，
你踏入林中。
童真的你，
遍尋百香果的種子。
秋天落滿你一身楓葉：
它們豐滿的色彩
鋪成迷宮般的仙境。
一片一片拾起，
通往記憶的地圖一一浮現：
每一瓣昨天，
每一道月亮和太陽的光亮，
甜蜜而憂傷，
突然間你長大了。
在秋天的鏡子上，這個流動的
閃閃發光的新世界，
你的指尖滑入，
旋轉再旋轉，
那些閃亮的星星……
你是那孩子，你又不是那孩子，
舀起來，

那些甜蜜，
那來自心靈的聲音，
召喚
每一次醒來……
你是那孩子，
那孩子是我。

A Dream

Into a forest,

you follow a sound.

The child you are,

searches for seeds of passion fruit;

instead, leaves of autumn fall over you.

Their rich colors

make a maze of wonderland.

Picking up one and another,

you see a map of lost memories.

Each drop of yesterday,

each light of moon and sun,

sweet and sad, suddenly you grow up.

On the autumn mirror, the

sparkling moving new world

that you have stepped in,

your fingertips slip into,

spinning shining stars…

The child you are, the child you are not,

scoop up,

the sweetness,

the song of a heart,

calling

to awake…

the child you are,

the child I am.

一定會有什麼

一定會有什麼
在那高高的山崗上；
當新月低語於陰影，
樹枝伸展它們的末梢，
貓頭鷹悄悄地停駐。

一定會有什麼
在輕輕的微風裡；
當潮濕的五月吐露芬芳，
窗口半開，
陽光送進金色的圖案。

一定會有什麼
在軟軟的沙灘上；
當日落吻別天邊，
波濤盤旋著泡沫，
細沙簇擁著我們的腳印。

一定會有什麼
在深深的積雪裡；
當寂靜籠罩著山巒，
松鼠緊緊抓住果核，
而我遠遠地看著你。

There Must Be Something

There must be something
upon the hill.
When new moon whispers to shadows,
trees stretch each limb,
and owls halt.

There must be something
in the breeze.
When Misty May breathes fragrance,
windows half-open,
sunrays shed gold.

There must be something
on the beach.
When sunset dips down the skyline,
tide spreads white skirts,
sand embraces our footprints.

There must be something
beneath the snow.
When quiet dominates mountains,
squirrels clutch pinecones,
I watch you from a distance.

住在房子裡的女人

你總在門口徘徊，
用兩種語言呼吸。

回憶就像房子有著前院，後院，
你卻想著多加幾個窗戶。
其實無所謂空間增值，
更沒有美化價值，
除了你住在這裡。

風把門彈來彈去──
影子在月光中打撈。

總有一天，你倦了。
掛牌等著房子出售。

在別處的故事，門背後
耳語不斷另一種語言。

他們不知道你去了哪兒──
而雨如簾子一樣，
裹在你的臉上。

愛的燈塔

The Woman within Her House

Around the doorway, you wander,
breathe in two languages.

Remembrance is a house
with front and back yards.
You want to add more windows.
Not for increasing its value,
nor to make it pretty.
Just because you live there.

The wind swings the door open—
shadows float in moonlight.

Someday you'll get tired
and list the house for sale.

But somewhere else, behind a door,
whispers imitate languages.

Nobody knows where you have been—
the rain is like a curtain,
your face veiled.

陌

通往她房間的門關上；
那裡有著整個世界。

第一次輕叩，他
留下一張紙條——
星星，帶我去航行。
她把他的字條折疊
成仙鶴。夜幕降臨。他
看到羽翼由線牽引
展向空中。

第二次輕叩，他
留下草帽在門口。
玫瑰一朵，嬌嫩蒼白
漸漸在其中凋謝。
拾起花瓣，她張貼在
鏡子上。
曙光照亮它們
就像太陽車輪。

第三次輕叩，他
帶來一條白的長絲巾——
大海的波紋揚起。
靜靜地，門開了。
蒙上彼此的眼睛，
他們走了進去。

The Path

The door to her room is closed;
there is a whole world there.

He knocks on it for the first time
and retreats with a note—
Stranger star, guide my sailing.
She folds his note into
a paper crane. Night falls. Hung
by strings, he sees its wings
up in the air.

The second time, he leaves
his hat at the door.
A rose fragile and pale inside
dies slowly.
She gathers the petals and mounts
them on her mirror.
The dawn light glows on them
like sun-wheels.

The third time, he brings
a long white scarf—
waves from an open ocean.
In silence, the door opens.
Blindfolding each other,
they enter the room.

深夜

今晚這只貓蹲在角落，
它哪也不去。
微眯的眼睛讓我不安。

粉色衣裙褪了一半，
膚色如雪，鏡子裡的
蒙娜麗沙笑了笑
突然有點遲疑。

轉過身，再轉，
慢慢停住，
牆角一隻蜘蛛，
悠然地蠶食
落網的飛蛾。

Late Night

The cat huddles in a corner.
Tonight he won't go anywhere.
His half-open eyes make me nervous.

My pink dress is half off,
skin shining like snow.
Mona Lisa in the mirror
smiles and hesitates.

Turning around and around,
I stop slowly.
A spider on the wall
enjoys a moth.

紅莓

平躺床上
我們像兩只比目魚。

窗外，星星更老了。

月亮這個白色的繭
在河面投下自己的影。

在稀疏的陰影中
柳樹單薄著搖晃。

沿著帶刺的欄杆
紅莓紅得流血。

她們記得
曾經像火一樣
吸引著畫蛾子
扇動翅膀
撲向愛情。

Raspberries

On our bed
we lie like flatfish.

Outside, stars grow older.

The moon, a white cocoon,
casts its image on the river.

In sparse shadows
a willow dangles.

Along the thorn fences
raspberries blced.

They remember
once being the fire
drawing the moth
flapping its wings
to flames of love.

讀特德修斯的月亮

月亮，我墜入了你的愛河。
看著你好似羞澀的藝術家
退回到夜幕裡。
聆聽著秋夜，你悄然
出來，手裡拎著一個圓桶。

月亮，他們都已離去。
獨留下你照看著
夜色裡的長河。
多少年過去了？
你看著小小的村莊
成為漂浮的島嶼。
在行行的窗戶之間，
黑夜流動，而我難以成寐。

我多想模仿李白，
依著他的長衫漫舞，
伴著燃燒的心輕唱。
每晚都來邀請你共飲。
美酒不會乾涸，

而李白沉沒在銀色的河水中，
再也不見身影。

月亮，提起你的圓桶，
再一次出來吧，
我會安靜得不弄出半點聲響。

After Reading Ted Hughes'
"Full Moon and Little Frieda"

I fall in love with you, Moon,

seeing you step back like a timid artist.

Listening to the night,

you come out, a pail lifted.

Moon, they are gone.

They left you watching over the river.

How many years since?

And you watch the small village

becoming a floating island.

Among rows of windows,

the night flows, and I'm wide awake.

How much I want to imitate Li Bai,

dancing with his white sleeves,

a humming from his burning heart,

night after night inviting you for a drink!

The wine never drained,

yet he drowned in the silver river.

Moon, lift your bucket,

come out once more.

I won't make a sound.

After Reading Ted Hughes' "Full Moon and Little Frieda"

蘋果和梨

除了蘋果，我對梨有別樣的感覺。
我在餐桌上擺放它們，卻捨不得品嘗。
漸漸它們從桌上退去，上了牆上的畫框。

偶爾它們出現在我的夢裡，
同時出現的一個是我親密的
愛人，另一個卻很陌生。
他們靠得很近，就像
在畫中，光澤輝映，陰影交疊。

透過深瞭的眼神，我不自禁伸出手，
卻每每夢醒。
水果的乳酸味就這樣
在清涼的夜色中蔓延。

Apples and Pears

In addition to apples,

I have a special feeling toward pears.

I place them on the kitchen table,

but fear to pare them.

Soon they retreat to the wall of my living room.

Occasionally appearing in my dreams

at the same time are my dearest lover,

and the other, a stranger.

They are close, like the pair of pears

in the painting, shadows overlapped.

My hands slip in the moonlight,

the bittersweet fruit flavor

spreads in the cool night.

石榴

我遞給你一盤水果。
你只要了一個石榴。
切開它，
我看到腥紅的籽。
你提取十二粒，
以同樣的方式吞下
如同　你兒子吞下藥丸……

他早已進入冥界，
沒有半點消息來回。
整整一年，你就像一座雕像，
塗抹著餘下的腥紅。

我不知道
該如何喚醒你──
如何衝破冥王的獄門？

我們等待種籽風乾──
發癢並流下腥紅淚滴……
匯成紅色的河流。
那時雪會降落，
覆蓋一切，一切
連同這個故事。

Pomegranate

I offer you fruit.
You only take a pomegranate.
Cutting it open,
I see the bleeding seeds.
You take twelve, swallow them
the same way your son swallows pills…

He goes into the Underworld,
no messages back and forth.
The whole year, you remain like a statue,
wearing the rest of the seeds.

I don't know
how to wake you up—
how to breach Hades' gates.

We wait for the seeds to dry out—
tickling red tears… red rivers…
then snow will cover
everything, everything
even this story.

一隻中國夜鶯

從這個視窗看出去，
一小片天空，高處，一片雲飄浮。
它的陰影下，一行行白楊
靜立；葉子都已落去，
纖薄的枝椏框構小小窗格。

裡面：冰冷如一口廢棄的水井，
深處布滿青苔。風吹進來
晃動著空空的蛛網。

窗臺邊
一隻夜鶯在低唱
他唯一的樂曲，
聲音嘶啞如沙沙飄落的樹葉。

我走近，伸出手掌，
金色的麥粒
如同貴重的誘餌——
來吧，拿去。
我喃語。

他轉身。
我看見我自己的影子，
如此沉重，無法拾起。

A Chinese Nightingale

From this window,

it is a patch of sky, up high, a cloud floating.

Beneath its shadow, poplar trees

stand tall in rows; leaves already fallen,

thin branches frame tiny lattices.

Inside: cold like an abandoned well,

deep, moldy. Winds blow in

and dangle empty webs.

By the window,

the bird sings his only song,

his voice drained as rustling leaves.

I approach, palms baited with

golden grains—

Come, take some.

I coo.

He turns.

I catch my own shadow,

too heavy to lift.

化妝舞會

原地轉圈，
我們成為舞池的落單者。
我們的道具更像沉默的宣言，
你執白，我執黑，
一局下到中盤的棋。

不斷地錯過快三，
慢四，我們還在執迷
為什麼而舞，以什麼而舞。
彷彿舞就是一種膠質，
無法逃離的窒息，
冰雨水火交錯在一起。

在我們站立的空隙裡，
風不停地拍擊
我們搖擺的棋。

Masquerade Party

Circling around the same spot,
we become lonely partners.
Our cover-ups make a silent statement:
yours in white, mine in black,
a Chess game.

Constantly missing Waltz,
and Foxtrot, we ponder
why and how we want to dance,
as if dancing is a collision
among fire and ice.

Between the lines
of where we stand,
the wind slaps us
like two torn pieces.

三步曲

*

陽光再現

影和我

同行

*

秋風撩起

葉和我

狂舞

*

窪中映射

樹與我

緊依

Three haiku

*

the sun coming out
shadow and I
walk together

*

blown by the wind
leaves and I
dance wildly

*

reflections on the puddle
the tree and I
lean closer

愛的迷惑

你愈想，它就愈像
一塊石頭，
躺下去，
你觸到它的冰涼。

仿如把春天挽進髮髻，
讓秋色泊在臉上──
一面冷寂的古老陶瓷。

風塵中，
一隻魚的眼睛盯著
你漂浮的夢，
睡蓮爬滿了池塘。

你深入微亮的岩洞
去尋找如火的真相，
和燃燒的火舌。

夜輾轉，
你抱緊它的冬天。

The Love Puzzle

The more you think, the more
it is like a rock.
Lying down,
you feel the coldness.

As if you have locked
spring beneath your hair bun,
autumn withers your face—
cool ancient china.

Through the dust,
a fish-eye stares
into your dream,
water lilies creep
on your pond.

You enter the depth
of a dim-lit cave
for its burning tongue
and flaming truth.

Night is quiet.
Sleepless,
you cuddle
the winter.

拾起一棵蒲公英

在黎明之前，
我拾起你，
將你拉近。
我的手指慢慢滾過
你的身體，
彈去附在你身上的種子，
將它們釋放到空中。

我聽到你的歎息
彷彿微風在山谷回漩。
透過車輪樣的晨光，
我看到你赤裸新鮮。
身影此刻薄如打開的繭，
臉開向天空，
然後轉向我，快樂地顫動。

Picking up a Dandelion

Before dawn,

I pick you up,

then bring you closer.

My fingers slowly roll

over your body,

removing seeds attached to you,

free them into the air.

I hear you sigh

as if breezes swirl at the bottom

of mountains. Through wheels

of twilight, I see you naked and fresh.

A shadow, and now a thin split cocoon,

your face opens to the sky,

then turns to me, shivering in joy.

我經常夢見魚

醒來卻驚異
自己的赤裸。

魚是性的一種象徵，
專家如是說；
神色中透著些古怪。

猶疑不安著，我記得
睡前卸下了所有行裝。

躺在愛人的身旁，
寧靜並熠熠閃光，
我的愛人是月下的河床。

只是，在我的夢裡，
沒有河流，也沒有水。
只有一尾發光的魚。

I Often Dream of Fish

Wake up surprised
by my nudity.

Fish is a symbol for sex,
a specialist explains;
she offers a miserable look.

Distressed, I remember
removing all belongings
before bed.

Lying beside my lover,
quiet and gleaming,
my lover is a river.

Yet in my dreams,
there is only one fish,
no river, no water.

靜物

一幅水果畫掛在
我們客廳的牆上
早晨的太陽很少眷顧，
只有昏睡的月亮來賞臉。

午夜醒來，
我發現自己的黑色輪廓
徘徊在那些等候的蘋果上。

我為它們痛惜，
不比在廚房盤子裡充當美味更好——
它們要麼面對刀子
要麼等著爛掉。

Still Life

A painting of fruit hangs
on the wall of our living room.
Morning sun seldom comes here.
Moon offers a drowsy face.

Awake at midnight,
I find my silhouette drifting
on the waiting apples.

I mourn for them,
no better than their succulence on a kitchen plate—
Either they face the knife
or wait to decay.

梵高的畫館

從向日葵，紫羅蘭
到麥田和星空，
我沉吟良久，
孤自一人聆聽。
我渴望畫家的筆
把我解剖成一道道光譜，
隱匿於某片畫布的角落，
從那裡我可以看著遊人以及自己
穿過不同的世紀，
為某種約定，某種情緒失色。

來自葵花深處，
我聽見嬰兒的啼哭
我不敢觸摸花瓶
的幽藍，儘管背景
滿是粉色。
而星空下，教堂的鐘樓
被黑暗籠罩，
鐘聲被地心力鎖住，
我發現自己站在畫室中心，
離每一幅畫都很遠
　　　　　　　　很遠。

注：「梵高」台譯「梵谷」。

In Van Gogh's Gallery

From sunflowers and violets
to the wheat field and starry sky,
I pondered and listened.
I longed for the painter's brush
to dissect me into slices of the light spectrum,
hidden in the corner of a canvas; from where
I could watch visitors and myself
through different centuries,
with some kind of agreement,
each face's color lost.

I heard a baby crying
from the depth of his sunflower.
I dared not touch the faint blue
vase, although the background
was lavish pink.
Under the stars, the church tower
cast shadows;
its chimes were choked by dark gravity.
I found myself standing in the center of the gallery.
Each painting seemed far
                              far away.

根雕

這棵樹在鋸聲中倒下，
不久就要連根拔起。
經一雙精巧的手慢慢雕鑿，
它重現地底下的蒼虯。

將死卻益發剛勁的枝，
逃過了無數次雷擊；
如今休憩於人們的頂禮，
凝成美和生命的定格。

轉身，我們捂緊被凍土
層層包裹的心，
一次次移植，
不為人觸摸的滄桑。

Root Carving

This tree falls
in echoes of the saw,
roots pulled up roughly.
Dedicated hands
chisel them until
their dragon facade appears.

Dying, once resilient limbs
surviving flashes of lightning,
now recline under sympathetic eyes.

Turning around,
we hold ourselves
in layers of cold, hard soil.
Transplant our roots—
hardship beyond anyone's touch.

幸運日子
——讀馬緹・爵威

他們喚你
幸運的女孩。
沒人知道
你很小心
拿捏自己的運氣。
——不要太多，
不然會跌入黑暗。

你經常夢見
一隻黑色的貓
但醒來瞥見
自己的身影——
眼睛閃亮，
急於跳出。

必須承認你的幸運——
及時撤退到陰影中……
一個影子製造商，
而不是飛蛾
去滿足撲火的輝煌。

未知仍然保持未知。
警報器粉碎了格溫多林的美夢。
幸運的是，你的生活，自己清楚——
以詩歌的方式。

Lucky Days
—*after Marty Gervais*

They call you
a lucky girl.
Nobody knows
you are careful
to pinch
your own luck
—not too much of it,
or else you must fall in the dark.

You often dream of a black cat
but wake up to catch
a glimpse of yourself—
irises so bright,
eager to jump out.

You admit your blessing
to retreat to shadows in time…
turning into a shadow maker,
not a moth toward fire.

The unknown remains unknown.

Sirens shatter Gwendolyn's dream.

With luck, a life you know—

the way of Poetry.

Note:

    Shadow Maker is the title of Rosemary Sullivan's Life of poet
Gwendolyn MacEwen

借來的故事

和你帥氣的父親相見已經太遲，
年輕的他早在戰爭中死去。
你冰箱門上，他滿臉笑容，
你卻滿臉憂鬱。
我想擁抱你，親吻你脆弱的眼睛；
但你已經長大了，
不是那個打電話的男孩
「回來吧，爸爸」──
這早已被遺忘的話，
從你的書中被我拾起。

這是一個借來的故事，
但我仍然感到內疚
為不能去觸擁你──
一個我夢中的小孩，
這些年來
我攜帶的霧重似黑珠。

也許，我是另一個孩子，
你不知道，也沒見過，或者聽過。

借來的故事沒有返回地址，
我只是又一個身影
在鏡子裡無從涉入……

有一天
你張開的手掌，
一滴清淚：
你的倒影，
我的複身，
終於相遇並且融化
慢慢擴散的
痛苦和快樂。

在那裡我們相會。

注：

　　斜體取自Dana Gioia（達納‧喬依爾）的詩「尋找寶盒中的家書」。

A Borrowed Story

Too late to meet your handsome father
who was wearing a new uniform
among other pilots, all from foreign countries,
all in their twenties, perished in the war.
What he left was only this photo—
seven decades now, stuck on your refrigerator door,
black and white, faces smile, yet yours somber.

I want to hug you, smooth your tousled hair,
hold your cold hands, read you a warm poem…
but you have already grown old, no longer the boy
who rose from nightmares and called:
"Come back, Dad!" —
a long-forgotten line,
I picked it up from your volume.

This is a borrowed story, foreign
but local to my mother tongue.
On this land where I landed
I feel guilty for not soothing you—
the child in my dream…
his wondering lonely eyes, all these years
the mists I've forever carried weigh like black pearls.

Perhaps, I am just one of the other kids,

        on the other shore of the ocean,

        you didn't know, never saw, or heard—

        who cried for her own father.

My letters to him have no address.

        He is yet another shadow

in the mirror

that has vanished…

One day on our open palms,

upon teardrops, the reflection

of us, the duplicates of our dads,

        finally meet and melt

as our slowly   diffusing

        pain and pleasure.

See you there!

note:

    The two italicized lines are from Dana Gioia's "Finding a Box of Family Letters."

探訪多大哲學系到戲劇系

找到你的辦公室時，我發現門上了鎖。
黏在門上的是你的
傳記書封皮，附帶名片
和空白的藍色日程表。
不甘心，我探尋著隔壁。似乎
屬於哲學系那種鼓搗疑惑的女教授，
有著長長的名字，我試想開倒車，
像電影一樣回溯。你一定明白
我的無奈，尋隱者不遇。

我是滿載而來，新鮮出爐的手稿，
手工書寫的，滿滿的。
我說的是我的心，自然你是
明白的亦或還是不懂。
我尋思如何道歉：
無意中打翻了一瓶香水，
現在它的香味無處不在，
「傾城」──名符其實。
大廳裡很安靜，沒有人查問。

在出口處，我拿起一份雜誌，
「當代」──免費：
電影評論和新劇討論。
我翻閱著，惶恐而驚訝：
高等學院的不設防的融入
幾近裸體，處處誘惑。

探訪多大哲學系到戲劇系

From the Department of Philosophy to Drama

I find your office, closed, of course.
A yellow dust cover is glued on your door,
a business card attached,
and a blue timetable remains blank.
I check the next door. The office seems to
belong to a female professor with a long name
and siren songs: two winged horses pulling a Chariot.
I have the urge to reverse my steps
like a film run backwards.
You must understand my disappointment.

Speaking of that, I have brought my new manuscript,
piles of handwriting. Calligraphic tadpoles
swim in the night river. full…
I mean, my heart as well, you know?
I must apologize—
accidently I knocked over a bottle of perfume,
and now its scent is everywhere,
"Allure" —according to its ad.
The hall is quiet and no one queries me.

At the exit, I pick up a magazine,

"Now" —for free.

Inside, film reviews and new drama.

I flip through it—

here, the surging desire:

human bodies, nearly naked, all lusting.

紀念張純茹

我還能堅持多久，
我能感覺到灰燼，
生命的歌唱不到盡頭，
我聽見風把它帶走？

什麼是空茫，
什麼是流連，
光陰是一架擺空的琴，
我聽不見鍵擊的樂音……

從我的手指滑落的，
是夢，抑或永生？
心是否追墜，
那不朽的靈魂？

注：張純茹，《南京大屠殺》等多本著作的作者。

愛的燈塔

Mourning for Iris Chang

How long will I hold up?
I feel your ashes around me.
Your song of life cannot be completed;
I hear the wind blow it away.

Time is an empty piano,
white and black, with a disturbed tune.

What slips through our fingers?
Beneath plum boughs,
petals shroud the ground
as last night's snow.

note:

    Iris Chang, an American--born Chinese journalist, author of
The Rape of Nanking.

多倫多，不再哭泣！
——紀念Cecilia Zhang

我夢見你深紅色，
日出如華彩絢麗，
楓葉如火燃燒無盡。

穿越銀色的絲線，你在航行，
透明的羽翼滑行在新月上，
而細雨霏霏閃著光亮。

下邊的城市被黃色的絲帶圍了起來，
裡面的街道在回憶中冷寂無聲，
細長的建築群蜷縮著沉默，
而人群四處搜尋著證據。

你微笑的海報，
被心碎的人們攜帶；
他們驅動四輪去追尋你，
遍歷著整座城市，
翻開每個陰暗的角落。

愛的燈塔

來臨的春天很冷，
淒冷如披露的新聞。
燭光和慰問卡滿載我們的思念，
衷心希望在天堂的你永遠安息。

你玉駕的彩虹滑進我的夢裡，
柔和的光亮注入我的詩裡。
星星在你的眼裡閃爍著，
在和諧的歌聲中一同升起。

疾風吹開我的眼淚，
氣流潤濕我的聲調；
天使在你的近旁，
帶領你走向永恆的天堂。

微風輕聲低徊，
沙灘慰撫海濤，
你躺下的地方將開滿鮮花，
傷害你的人必將受到懲罰。

願風帶來你的芬芳，
願鳥歌唱你的曲調，
願愛人們編織你的夢，
願無家的人找到你的燈籠。

我用詩句噴繪我的夢境，
細磨憂傷出離我的心靈。
我的聲音在海嘯中回蕩，
「多倫多，不再哭泣！」

Toronto, No More Weeping
—in memory of Cecilia Zhang

I dream of you in crimson,
morning sun blazing in its glory,
maple leaves flaming on the skyline;

Through silvery threads you are sailing,
sheer wings gliding upon the crescent,
with drizzle drifting in its glowing.

The city below railed off by yellow ribbons,
streets inside muted in cold reminiscence.
The slim buildings huddle in silence,
as crowds hunt for evidence.

They spin their wheels to chase you,
plough shadows of each angle.
Your smiling posters traverse the entire city
carried by the heartbroken.

The coming spring is very cold,
even as chilly as the breaking news.
Candles and cards confide our yearning
wish for you to reside in peace in heaven.

You ride on a rainbow to my dream;
pour soft light upon my poem.
Starlets gleaming in your eyes,
rise up in primal unison.

Whirlwinds brush away my tear,
streams moisten my tone.
The angel, a presence very near,
walks you into the eternal heaven.

Breezes wave their rustle.
Beaches cradle their ocean.
Where you lay shall burst into rich blossoms.
Whom you suffered by, shall pay for the crime.
May winds bring in your fragrance.

May birds sing in your tune.

May loved ones weave your dreams.

May the homeless find your lantern.

I paint my dream with each line,

and hone the blues off my mind.

My voices echo with tsunami howling,

"Toronto, no more weeping!"

罪惡之城

在這裡我可以愛上
一條斑斕燦爛的蛇。
我虛空的靈魂渴望時尚，
漸漸淡化在漣漪鏡子裡。

在誘惑之中迷失。
沒什麼大不了。
一切都披戴無窮的色彩。
每一色彩沾染著魅力。

在光焰的虹彩裡，蛇
吞下天空。
伊甸園的樹倒下。

我是留下還是離開？
我的皮囊越發輕薄。
戀棧在有罪的愛裡，
我成為罪人。

太陽把自己變成
　　一個巨大的熾熱的蘋果。

The Sin City

Here, I could fall in love
with a splendid snake.
My plain soul longs for style
and fades into a rippling mirror.

It is fine to get lost
among enticements
Everything wears infinite hues,
each speaks volumes of glamour.

In gleaming colors, the snake
swallows the sky.
The tree from the Garden falls.

Will I stay or leave?
My skin is thinner,
I battle with the love of sin,
and become sinful.

The sun turns itself
      into a giant sizzling apple.

一式兩份

這幾天你沉迷跡象：
桌上，一套藍色的瓷器，
窗邊，一個空蜘蛛網。
頭頂，一朵浮雲，
外形無法命名，
而一陣風過──鹹熱──
來自東方或西方？

你在睡眠中行走迷宮。
東西沒有丟失。
你手裡的紅色和金色的書，
隱藏著藍：
不要指望你會
在別人的夢裡留下線索。
迷宮掩蓋著的綠色出口。

你持有的一切──雖然小──
但無法返回仍然會悲傷。
你想複製它們：
鑰匙，指針，心肝和愛。

因為如果出錯一次，
那麼愛人，至少，
還有另外一份
可以擁持。

一式兩份

In Duplicate

"Beware of things in duplicate" — *Dana Gioia*

These days you read for signs:
on a table, a set of blue china,
at the window, a spider's web…
Over your head, a floating cloud,
shape hard to name,
then a sudden gust—hot and salty—
from the east or west?

You sleepwalk in a maze.
Nothing is lost.
The book you hold in red and gold
conceals blue:
Do not expect that you have left
threads in others' dreams.
The maze disguises its green exit.

Everything you hold—so small—
still hurts when not returned;
you wish to duplicate it:
keys, hands, hearts, and love…

For if a mistake is made,

then you, at least,

have another

to hold.

風景

讓我傾讀你的手心
找尋某個季節的風景。

讓我繫一根金色的絲線
在這個迷宮的夢幻裡
通過綿長的走廊
在褪色群星中
到達你的綠色核心。

可是我不過一尾魚，
絕望地渴求空氣。
空氣很熱。
你穿著一件秋天的毛衣。

在這片大地上，
我褪落夏天的偽裝
周旋於落葉圈中。
我們頭頂同樣一個天空。
一棵樹深秋中。

離開時，
我記起冬天突然降臨
雪花落下。

Landscape

I want to read your palm
to seek a seasonal landscape.

I long to tie a golden thread
in this labyrinth of dreams
through the winding hall
among fading stars
to your green core.

But I am a fish,
desperate for air.
The air is hot.
You wear your autumn sweater.

In this land,
I shed a summer layer
and swirl in a circle of leaves.
There is a sky above us.
A tree in late autumn.

On departing,
I recall a sudden winter
snow falls.

石蓮

在玻璃器皿裡，
園藝師鋪上黑白相間
的沙子和石粒，
再插上小小的綠葉豐碩的植物，
說，這就是石蓮。

我是拿好酒換來的，
看似毫不起眼的，聖誕禮物。
只為那綠意融融的蓮狀，
和黑白沙粒彌漫的浪漫。

如果愛是一種病，
等待則是苦藥。
手心接滿晨光中的露水
我將其慢慢澆灌。
在玻璃器皿之上，
那蓮的心事，誰懂？

The Houseleek (Sempervivum)

In a square terrarium,

the gardener spreads

sand and stone grains

in white and black,

then plants a green leafy plant;

he says, this is a houseleek.

I exchanged it for a bottle of wine—

a Christmas gift,

although seemingly trivial,

its lush jade lotus shape

beyond black and white

brings me a tiny bright hope.

If love is a disease,

waiting is the bitter medicine.

In the morning light,

collecting dewdrops with my fingertips,

I slowly drip each on the plant.

Above the terrarium,

who else appreciates

the heart of a houseleek?

立冬

當落葉把最後的輝煌歸還大地，
一朵白雲靜若處子
在斑斕的湖面倒映。

旅行的人會暫時停下，
湖面翻滾著熱浪，
時空就像綠茶，倒出來
滿湖的芬芳。

品上一口，在進入冬眠之前，
讓流水的回聲在心裡回蕩，
然後一葉一葉展開
在夢裡的旅程。

Beginning of Winter

When fallen leaves
return their final glory to the earth,
a white cloud, quiet and demure,
reflects in the gorgeous lake.

Travelers pause to ponder—
the lake rolling warm waves.
Spacetime is like green tea,
pouring out all of its fragrances.

Sip it before hibernation begins.
Let echoes of the river resound,
then unfold one leaf after another
toward a journey in dreams.

我在心中築了一個雪人

一場雪後，
這世界並沒有變得純淨，
很快恢復原來的本色。
光禿的還是光禿，
泥濘的還是泥濘。
雪花落在我的臉上
和手上，來不及去捕捉，
那美麗匆匆逝去。
在路的盡頭，
我開始在心中
築著一個雪人，
我把他安放，說，
這裡是你的家，我們相伴。

入夜了，空氣變得很冷，
我無法久留，也無法帶他入室。
好想擁抱著告別，
卻擔心雪人他會融化消失，
只好揮揮手，
讓晚安輕輕飄過。

在另一個夢幻世界，
那裡很多雪人，
那裡世界如此純淨，
我也變成一個雪人。

我在心中築了一個雪人

I Build a Snowman in My Heart

After snowing,

this world has not become pure,

it swiftly reverts to its old look.

Bareness is still bare.

Muddiness still remains muddy.

Snowflakes fall on my face

and on my hands.

Before I catch them,

they melt away and leave no beauty.

At the end of the road,

I start to build a snowman in my heart.

I lay it down and say:

Here is your home.

We now accompany one another.

Night falls, it gets cold,

I cannot stay longer,

no way to bring him inside.

I want to embrace him with a goodbye,

but fear that he will melt and disappear,

I only can wave my hand

and say my Goodnight.

In another dreamy world,

I see many snowmen,

and the world is so pure,

I also become a snowman.

給歐文・萊頓

經過這麼多年，
你是否還是相信
詩歌存在僅僅在於證實靈魂的黑暗？

當最後的一個女人
（那你不曾問起名字或早已遺忘）
離你而去，你是否會譜寫不一樣的情詩？
你會不會後悔過往，
沒有什麼可以延續
除了粗糙昏暗地做愛？

萊頓先生，我嘗試著想像
你冷酷的一張臉，無情的一對眼睛。
只是最終我還是描繪你
混血，帶著深藍，淺紅和純白。

我想要相信
所有這些都是原生在你的血脈
和你的本性衝動中。
我想要向你呈現相異的經歷：
在詩歌找到我之前，
我幾乎被黑暗淹沒。

For Irving Layton

After so many years,
do you still believe
Poetry merely exists for showing the dark of our soul?

Would you write love poems differently
after your last woman left you
(many of them vanished without a name)?
Would you regret that nothing remained
behind the rugged and dark sex?

Mr. Layton, I try to picture you
a cold face with bold eyes.
But I always end my painting
with mixed blue, red and white.

I want to believe
all these are in your veins
and your impulses.
I long to show you the opposite:
Before poetry found me,
I was nearly drowned in dark.

傳奇

一束光穿過黑暗的屋子，
你在那獨自等待，
手裡握著一面鏡子，
光經過並轉向
光痕記載下來。

一條河穿過荒漠，
種子早埋在那裡，
季風過後，一片綠洲形成
你看到芳華被帶往
更遙遠的地方。

一本書在我們的眼裡
打開，不斷改寫……
月亮投下變幻的臉
在平靜的湖面上，
我們等待
吹皺的一江春水。

The Lord of Light

A beam of light went through the dark room,
you waiting there, a mirror in your hand;
the light passed by and turned around
and its track was recorded.

A river ran through the desert
where seeds were buried earlier.
Seasons went by, an oasis was created;
you watched winds carrying the green far.

A book opened before our eyes
and journeys were rewritten…
The moon lowered her changing face
on the lake;
we waited for ripples in spring river.

聖誕願望
——給萊昂納德・科恩

緊煨溫暖的爐火旁，
遠離田野和積雪，
我聲聲禱告，
一千個吻深深
穿越海面……
「你回到布吉街」。

流水緩緩恰如不斷交談。
你低沉的旋律陪伴長夜。
透過馬賽克，燈影閃爍。
雪花飄遠，美夢褪色。

陣陣寒風吹散片片樂譜，
仿如年輕的我緊緊追隨……
打開門，我注視良久，
然後轉身將門輕輕關上。

A Christmas Wish

—for Leonard Cohen

By a warm fire, away from the fields
and the whiteness, I send a prayer,
wishing a thousand kisses deep
down the sea…
"You are back on Boogie Street."

The water drops like a conversation.
Your melody boils over the slow night.
Windows exhale mosaic lights.
Snowflakes swirl in faded dreams.

Winds blow fragments of music sheets,
the girl in me, runs after…
I open the door and take a long look
then return to close it.

情人節
——恰讀火星移民計劃破產

每一次把玫瑰花瓣收集，
還有那落髮以及融化的雪，
每一次撫平眼角的皺紋，
以及心的悸動，
穿山越水，過了本命年，
這一次知命了，
卻笑得更燦爛無邪。

每一次執意於詩和遠方，
在夜的星空和夢的海洋，
在時空之上，穿越星際，
隨月船去漂流，
為著那永恆的對視
和天籟的絕唱。
穿山越水，過了本命年，
卻發現生命的盡頭，
愛的燈塔，不在遠方，卻在心中。

所以這一次，你早早地
翻開珍藏的書頁，傾情於文字
書寫久久回蕩的心意，
為生命中的每一次遇見和分離
為旅途上的每一個愛人和戀人
送上淡淡的花香和滿滿的祝福。

Valentine's Day

—reading news about Mars One Plan failed

Each time you collect rose petals,

fallen hair and melting snow.

Each time you smooth wrinkles

that loom at the corners of your eyes,

and calm down your fast heartbeat…

Crossing mountains and wading rivers,

after another round of birth years,

this time, you know life better,

and smile calmly and innocently.

Each time you insist on poetry and the far.

In the night sky and among oceans of dreams,

beyond time and space, through stars,

you drift with a moon boat

to search for the eternal vision

and the swan song of heaven…

Crossing mountains and wading rivers,

after another round of birth years,

you find that at the end of life,

愛的燈塔

Love's lighthouse is not in the distance,
but in your heart.

So this time, in advance, you
open the book and write on each page
with a long-lasting song,
for every encounter and farewell in your life,
for each lover and beloved on the journey
you send scent of roses and heartfelt blessings.

我的口音

它是迷人的。
我向你保證。
我也這樣保證自己，
並且選擇相信如此。

語言有各種顏色，
我想展示我柔和的藍。
但你的刀叉切下去，
比我的筷子點擊更快。

我的口音長成樹木，
小陌和蜿蜒的道路
通往西海岸的風景。
它指向敞開的天空；
但雲層沉重
並形成雨滴。

我的書頁收集他們
卻在沉默中風乾。
很多次在開口之前

我猶豫良久。
現在它生出牙齒。
即使加雜著齒距，
我決定
──這是我的聲音。

My Accent

It is charming.
I assure you,
I assure myself;
and choose to believe so.

Languages have colors.
I want to show you my tender blue.
But you cut off with fork and knife,
quicker than my chopstick taps.

My accent grows trees,
trails and winding roads to
westcoast landscape.
It points to the open sky;
yet clouds are too heavy
and form raindrops.

My papers collect them
then dry in silence.
I have hesitated many times

before speaking;

now it develops teeth.

Even with gaps between,

I decide

       —this is my voice.

生命瓶罐

當我還是孩子，
我被告知
寧靜就像光亮
有著顏色和面孔。

在黑暗中穿行鄉村，
我習慣了用螢火蟲裝滿一個玻璃瓶。
它成為我藍色的星星指南針。
當我吸進寧靜，
我能聽到輕微的聲音來自眾生，
每一個都在為一份生命歌唱。

成長以後，
穿行在這繁忙的城市之旅，
我想我們的生活罐子裡一定充滿著瑣事和雜訊；
然而，漫步於這個城市的山谷中，
我能感覺到寧靜，寧靜，寧靜——
這靜默就像陽光一樣
打開著一扇門。

沿湖岸行走，
我看到在水面上夕陽安靜的投影
遠航燈塔默默地增添它的輝煌。

一隻白色小天鵝
緩緩展翅……
我深吸這份安詳。

Life Jars

When I was a child,
I was told
silence is like light,
having colors and faces.

Walking through the country in the dark,
I used to fill a glass jar with fireflies.
It became my green starry compass.
When I inhaled the silence,
I could hear quiet voices from living creatures,
each making music of its own life.

Now grown up,
every day's busy journey in this hectic city,
I thought our life jars must be full of mundane trifles and noises;
Yet wandering into ravines in this urban landscape,
I can find the silence, silence and silence—
Where it opens a door like sunrays breaking through.

Riding along the lakeshore,

I see sunset's serene reflection on the lake,

the CN Tower topping its splendor.

A baby swan

          takes off…

I inhale the silence.

晚安

穿越那些黑色的夜晚
夢就像回家
找到自己的鑰匙，
打開門進入。
你起身，點好燈籠，
翻開書頁，相擁而坐，
四目對視，宛如
鏡子裡的寫真。
一陣低語，一陣輕風，
心就插上了翅膀，
從窗口飛出去，
去到那山水間，
那雲霞處，那楓林裡。
聽，流水在唱，石頭也在唱……
隨著螢火蟲，那月光下
的原野，處處天籟之聲。
你靜靜地等待
那顆屬於自己的星星，
在那些遙遙相望的星際中
仍然幻想著的孩子之間，

夢就像回家，
穿越那些黑色的夜晚
尋找自己的鑰匙。

Goodnight

Through dark nights
like coming home
dream finds his own key,
unlocks the door and comes inside.
You get up and light up the lantern;
sit with him and open the book.
Looking at each other, a pair in the mirror.
A whisper passes by, a breeze goes through…
Your heart grows wings,
flying out of the window
to where mountains are green,
clouds are shining, and maples are red.
Listen, the river sings, stones sing too…
Following fireflies, under the moonlight
the meadow rises with music from heaven.
Quietly you wait for the star you belong to.
Among distant stars and innocent children,
dream finding his own key
through dark nights
comes home.

愛的燈塔

*攝影、設計│管濤

愛的燈塔

故鄉的風

Winds from Hometown

那些老歌呀
我的心飄蕩
在月亮河畔

old songs…
my heart goes on
along the moon river

*攝影｜岑賢道

父親的家譜圖

紙上的一小點墨蹟，
在父親的眼裡長出青綠的枝椏。
吸著長長的煙袋，
暮色中，
父親勾畫滿腹的身世。

我可以感覺他的微笑，
在枝葉沉澱的鬱香中
漸漸綻放。
而今他最鍾愛的
在他的筆下煜煜生輝。

兒子，年輕有為的高級軍官
女兒，備受尊敬的知名學者
（父親極盡描摹著細節，就像母親
精心裝飾著聖誕樹）
然後，我，新興詩人。

父親並不認識詩人，
對他而言，「新興」多少有點苦樹皮的味道。
（我可以感覺到他筆的停滯）
而後，在「我」的邊上浮現
一顆亮亮的晶體
鮮明地映射出「海外工程師」注釋。
父親最後的揮毫，
像是庇護異鄉的「我」，
免於日子清貧地晾曬。

卷起這張微亮著的筆墨，
我把溫暖留在胸間——
某年豐收後，
從層層蠶繭的心，
我要抽出新的卷軸。

My Father's Family Tree

It all started from an ink spot,
my father took it as a sprouting bud.
Sucking on his pipe,
he drew his long narrative
on a piece of paper.

I can sense his smile,
as leaves spread their dense fragrance:
always his favourite,
now highlighted by a brush—
son: a high-ranking officer,
daughter: a respectable scholar,
(my father decorated each with details
like my mother's Christmas tree),
then me, the would-be poet.

My father has never known poets,
and, to him, "would-be" is worse than rough bark.
(I can feel his pause)
then, a tinted soft orb beside me:

"engineer abroad" perfectly mirrored.
My father ensured his final touch
to free me from starving.

I roll up this glowing paper,
and place its warmth on my chest—
Someday at harvest,
out from the chrysalis of my heart,
I shall start a new scroll.

雪

——給姐姐

這真是奇蹟。
醫生告訴我們
你不會等到雪季。
但今年，在我們溫暖的南方
冬天來得特別早。
我們急著從衣櫃中取出毛皮大衣，
既高興又擔心——
沒有人能預測試天氣和未來。
新聞報導，某個地方出現
從未有過的洪水，
另一個卻反常乾涸。
當我們年輕的時候，
我們是如此期待下雪。
尾隨著你，我們爭做雪天使，
我的總是最小。
天堂會下雪嗎？
沒有人告訴我們。
你說，那些走在我們前面的
是去察看。
並給我們留位。

Snow

—for my sister

It must be a miracle.
The doctor told us
you wouldn't make the snow season.
But this year, in our warm south
winter comes earlier.
We rush to get fur coats from closets.
We are both happy and worried—
no one can predict the weather
and the future any more.
In the news, somewhere where
there are never floods;
now it is under deep water.
When we were young,
we waited for snow eagerly.
Following you, I made snow
angels, mine always smaller.
Does it snow in heaven?
Nobody tells us.
Those who go before us, you say
go to check
and save a place for us.

因為風的緣故

故鄉的白楊
瘦成一排影，
空曠的枝
潛入我的夢。

我只有滿懷的楓葉，
剛剛落下，
帶著我手的餘溫。

它們低低傾訴，
一整個夏，餘蔭深深。

我把它們帶進溫室。
一葉一葉地裁剪，
衣裙一樣盛開在
我裸露的心房。
我想像　它們需要溫暖。

而秋色已停不住腳步，
泊進漆黑的夜。
我豎成一夜的燈柱，
不斷旅行的光
照亮了多少前路，
我反覆告訴自己——
冬天來了，春天還會遠嗎？

Because of the Wind

The poplars in my hometown
as slim as shadows,
bold branches
sneak into my dream.

Yet I have full hands of maple leaves
just fallen
with my body warmth.

They rustle quietly,
reminiscing of summer shade.

I carry each into my room,
sew them one after another.
Dressing them on my naked skin
I imagine they desire warmness.

Yet the fall cannot stop its footsteps,

and descends into the cold night.

I stand like a beacon.

Light travels to shine on the faraway road.

I repeat to myself —

If winter comes, can

Spring be far behind?

暮影

秋末，風卻溫暖如春。
我獨自漫步，想起昨夜手指劃破……
慢慢地，宣紙上紅玫瑰朵朵。

如果有一個信使，
你應該知道青春的影子
不是虛空——
仍然披紅戴綠，
儘管葉子落了，樹也依舊沉默。

曾經追逐曠野螢火，
現在暮光閃爍附近。
告訴我，智者，冬天是否白色的童話？
我渴望雪花滑落如你的話語，
精緻細膩，融化在我的舌尖。

夜幕降臨，
掌心，一江春水

Shadowlight

The autumn gusts feel warm
as if it's spring.
I walk alone and recall
last night by accident I cut my finger...
slowly, on the rice paper, red roses grew.

If there is a messenger,
we should know the shadow
of our youth isn't void —
I still wear warm colors,
although, leaves withered,
the tree grows silent.

Once I chased fireflies for Greenlight.
Now the blue twilight flickers near.
Tell me, sage, if the coming winter is a white tale.
I long for snowflakes as your words,
delicate and fine, melting on my tongue.

The night descends.
Upon my palm, a river flows.

致李清照

我用一襲藍火，
緊扣你的影子；
穿過大洋彼岸，
風的味道更鹹。

白是戚白，戚白的……
冷是淒冷，淒冷的……
在這初秋，我無法
向那些帶著口音
讀你詩的老外解釋。
他們追逐著問我：
我們這些腳步不留聲音，
雲鬢輕挽的中國女子，
為何避開陌生人。

哦，雲在我們頭頂。
我留意到墨蹟
落在我的肌膚上──
一絲月亮的痕跡。

For Li Qing Zhao

I cup your shadow
with blue fire;
across the ocean,
the wind tastes more salty.

The white is whiter,
and whiter...
the cold is colder,
and colder...

In the early autumn,
I fail to explain to those
who read your poems in accents.
They chase me with questions—
how we Chinese women,
footsteps no sound,
hairbun so high,
shy away from strangers.

Well, clouds are overhead.
I catch ink drops
on my skin—
a trace of moon.

你會是什麼植物呢？

心理諮詢師留下我們獨自
在房間裡，白紙散落
在桌子上。一瞬間
我們變得安靜起來。

我記得小時候
我畫了很多的蒲公英——
早晨的太陽下，它們自由
呼吸，等待趁風啟航。

現在，天暗下來。
夕陽投下了最後的一道光亮。
我的紙片上沒有蒲公英，
它們的種子可能散落某片荒蕪地。
也沒有玫瑰。它們要不了多久
就會暗淡乾枯。

我讀過一首仙人掌樹的詩——
醒目得獨樹一幟，但沙漠，
饑渴和荊棘我無法忍受。

我想我更喜歡果樹。

在我們的後院，有梨和蘋果。

雖然等不到它們的甜蜜，

（蟲子和鳥永遠搶在我們前面），

我也不會抱怨——

自然自有安排，畢竟，

蜜蜂和蝴蝶擔當了所有的工作。

你看，很可能我只是一棵松樹

至少松樹每個季節都會

圍護你的小空間；

然而，在我的紙上，鉛筆

畫了一圈又一圈

一層又一層

那是緊裹著

玻璃洋蔥。

你會是什麼植物呢？

Which Plant Are We?

The therapist leaves us alone,
papers scattered
on the table. Suddenly
we become quiet.

I remember when I was a kid
I drew lots of dandelion clocks—
beneath the morning sun, they breathe
freely, ready to take a windy ride.

Now it is getting dark.
The sunset casts its last light
on my paper. No dandelions.
Their seeds might land somewhere barren.
No roses either. They would turn
dark and dry over time.

I've read a poem about cactus trees:
so striking and so enticing, but the desert,
the thirst and the thorns are too hard to bear.
I decide I prefer orchards.

In our back yard, there are pears and apples.
But they never grow sweet to eat,
worms and birds are always ahead of us.

I think I had better be a pine—
at least an ideal fence.
On my paper my pencil
circles and circles -
layers and layers
of a glass onion.

河流向哪？

你已長大，
不再是牽著我衣角的
小女孩；
飄著蘆葦的河岸，
風還是那麼輕柔嗎？
沒有人再追著問，
河流向哪？

寄來的家信裡，
透露著變遷，
你沒有提及即將的婚禮，
只是懇求採幾簇楓葉。
遙遠的光焰編織在想像裡，
距離不能阻隔你的夢……

可以寄回秋色嗎？
還是青藤纏繞的詩篇？
這樣的季節，
看得見節節攀沿的追問，
和步步丈量的旅程……

Where Did the River Meander?

You are grown up,
no more the little girl following me
dragging on my sleeves.
Reeds once waved on the river banks,
I wonder, are winds still gentle?
Where did the river meander?
Now no one asks after me.

Letters from my hometown
have disclosed huge changes.
You didn't mention your wedding ring,
but asked for red maple leaves.
The quilted faraway flames in your imagination—
distance could not block your dream.

Could I mail back the color of autumn
or a poem entwined with vines?
This season,
I see long traces of my nostalgia
and hear question after question…

祖母的警告

星光很遙遠，
那些傳說又一次被提起。
只是所有的都是過去式，
和改寫過的名冊。

我們只是淡水魚，更貼切的，
沒有游泳證，困在魚缸的魚。
屬於天空的羽翼掛在夢裡，
那裡有很多國度，在詩歌中
沒有簽證必要。

你們可以想像我們有很多的
話語，裝在氣泡裡，
彩色的斑斕，升得最高
也是最輕巧的，如此容易破滅。
那些沉下去的像泥鰍的黝黑，
如龜殼的堅硬，是我們息息相存
的唇齒。

愛的燈塔

而你們，輕漫地議起我們，
以為自己是堅實的城牆
以及鮮明的旗杆，
在黑暗襲來的時候，
海藻一樣嚮往著飛翔。

Grandma's Warning

The legends of stars are told again,
but all in a past tense with a rewritten range.

We are just fresh-water fish—
no swim permitted,
trapped in this water tank.
Wings are hanging in dreams
where there are many countries
to traverse—with light.

We do have much to say, all
sealed in bubbles,
gorgeous colours, the higher they rise
the less they weigh, and the easier to burst.
What sinks to the bottom, dark as loaches,
hard as shells, are our lips and teeth—
closed and intact.

Yet never refer to us as thin-finned,
and think of yourselves as solid walls
and straight flagpoles;
when night falls,
we all sway like seaweeds
longing to fly.

家庭相冊

他們敘說——
我的哥哥，一匹黑馬，在夢想中奔跑，
從農村到城市，無數看不見的障礙——
我的兄弟，懷著白馬的夢。

他們歎息——
我的姐姐，一棵李樹，挖掘深厚的根基準備收成
惡劣的天氣和土壤貧瘠辜負了她，
我的姐姐，被冬天的松枝包裹。

他們指認——
我的父親，一頭金色的獅子，
身懷王國不斷翻滾咆哮——
但黑暗降臨，視力喪失，
我的父親，沉默的羔羊。

他們發誓——
我的母親，一座木頭房子，
穿過窗戶瞭望霧濛濛的道路。
當誘惑充滿危險，

關上門，她細細傾聽——
我的母親，夜晚的安息處。

而我，一隻醜小鴨，身著外國語的外衣，
一朵蒲公英，帶著自由飛翔的意志，
一把鋒利的剪刀，切下紙的陰影，
一棵睡蓮，追逐幻想。

Family Album

They say—
my brother, a black horse, trotting amid dreams,
from countryside to city with myriad invisible hurdles—
my brother, a dreamer of Pegasus.

They sigh—
my sister, a plum tree, digging deep roots for full-loaded
    fruit –
the harsh weather and poor soil fail her,
my sister, a winter pine closing up.

They state—
my father, a golden lion,
with a kingdom in mind; rolling and roaring –
the darkness descends, with sight lost,
my father, a silent lamb.

They swear—
my mother, a wooden house,
with windows peering through the foggy road.

When too tempted outside,

closing the door and learning to listen—

my mother, a hut for night.

And I, a grey duck, dressing in a foreign skin,

a dandelion clock, flying with a free will,

a sharp scissors, cutting paper shadows,

a water lily, setting out for fantasy.

＊攝影、設計│管濤

七夜之十二生肖

（一）

並不像你其他的夢：
在一輪純淨圓潤的月下，
一條蒼翠的龍安靜馴服。
你伴著葉子沙沙聲入睡；
頭額上頂著晶瑩的露珠。

這是一個冬季，
處處頻臨冷凍極地——
沉重的冰柱懸掛，
富麗的陽光炫耀……
一尾快凍結的蛇
嘶著寒冷和白霧。

她渴望挺立並散發光亮，
軀體盤旋而上，
舌頭彈射——
　　　　炙熱，危險。

（二）

一匹黑馬跑進你的夢裡……

　　　　轉身停下；
你站在角落
　　　　巨大的花瓶旁。

他嗅著花瓶口，
你記得你藏在那裡
的口信，早已隨風飄散。

你懇求，
離開吧。
這裡是廢棄的房子……

他低頭，
舔舐你的手，
鼻子朝向西方，
　　緩緩地踢著馬蹄。

你睜開眼睛——
　　月光從窗口洩下……
冬季的花園
　　　馬早已褪成白色。

這裡，你獨自一人多年。
那兒，他光禿著，在雪裡。
日落贈你一襲紅色的袍子，
黑夜將它奪走。

（三）

你看到自己身上
　　　　　　長滿白色的蒲公英
徜徉在山間……

牧羊人召喚圈地遊戲
「雙眼緊閉……」

　　　雙眼緊閉

多年來，你一直遵守這一教條
多年來，你浸沒在這藍色星球裡
　　　並且倖存下來

你看見蒲公英被拔起……
　　種子飄向空中
　　在別處落下

（四）

鳳凰樹不再
收攏鬱鬱蔥蔥的枝椏，
蜷縮其下的是只白虎。

秋霜覆蓋大地——
豐潤的果實被一掃而空。

你退居於一座白色的房子。
白色的窗框裡，
白色煙霧繚繞。

一隻受驚的玉兔躍起⋯⋯
月亮蒼白的臉回望。

（五）

洪水滔滔。
天黑下來。
江河上漲。

你聽到龍的雷鳴聲。
樹木倒下，山坍塌。
猴子尖叫著四處奔散。

在一座巨大的屋頂上，
一隻公雞頻頻打鳴，
他的頭冠鮮紅無比：

不要慌張。
方舟一定到來。

（六）

到處都是白色和死寂，
你聽到公牛的呻吟。

環顧四周，
一頭粉紅色的豬低語：
公雞正躺在隔壁的房間裡——
有人切斷了他的喉嚨。

一條黃狗衝進來
想要拍照——
一隻黑貓緊跟著驅逐。

龍戴上一具碩大的面具，
老虎測量著自己的血壓。

警猴護送著一隻西裝革履的老鼠，
前擁後繼的是他的克隆兄弟。
老鼠輕咳一聲——

細長的鬍鬚讓你想起
卡通電影中一句名言：
「所有夢想都會成真。」

（七）

一棵藍色的樹從花瓶中彈出，
頂部開著七朵白色的玫瑰。

你的手碰觸
每一朵像雪花散落……

蛇爬進花瓶裡，
尾巴懸在外面。

光滑的瓶身映著
　　斷裂肋骨的
　　破碎陰影

你驚醒……

Seven Nights with the Chinese Zodiac

I

it isn't as in your other dream —
under a white bone-eyed moon
a green dragon quiet and tame;
you sleep with the Time Tower,
crowned by detached diamonds…

it is a winter season—
everywhere falls into *polar vortex* freeze
heavy icicles hang, flashing sunlight's glory…
an ice snake breathes cold and white

you long to rise and glow
body spiraling like a mountain road
tongue flicking—

            dangerous and hot

II

a dark horse runs into your dream...

he stops and turns...
in the corner, a huge vase
stands by you

he sniffs the edge...
you remember you hid notes
there, gone with fire and wind

you plead
this is a ruined garden...
leave!

he lowers his head
licks your hands
nose pointing to the West...
he kicks his hooves

you open your eyes

moonlight pours in…

here you are, alone, for seasons

there he is, bare, in snow…

sunset gifts you a red gown—

                    night takes it

III

you roam in hills…

enclosed by dandelion clocks

your shepherd calls to his circle game—

"make yourself blind…"

                           blind

for years, you've followed the advice

for years, you've survived this blue planet

your finger tracing a forbidden city…

        clocks plucked out

    weightless wings

              carry seeds…

IV

the phoenix tree in the Summer Palace
no longer gathers its lush branches—
curling up under it is a white tiger

autumn fires burn over the enormous land
abundant fruit has been swept away

you stare at a white house…
white smoke lingers
among white-framed windows

the startled jade rabbit leaps…
a white moon looks back

V

the sky descends
the river rolls

in this closing-up world,
the dragon thunders behind hefty clouds
the earth quivers
the towers fall down

> *Everywhere is the wild lament*
> *of lost souls.* *

on the roof of a historic site
a rooster crows repeatedly:

> *Don't be afraid.*
> *A boat will be provided.* **

his crown becomes stunningly red

VI

into the huge vase, you fall—
on a looking-glass
…shattered scales

pigs retreat into dark woods
oxen gaze at the broken window—
the rooster is dying with his throat cut

paparazzi rush in
cats chase them away

the dragon wears a giant mask
the tiger measures his own blood pressure

the police-monkey escorts a well-suited rat
followed by his cloned brothers
the rat makes a soft cough
his thin whiskers toss off a line

from a cartoon film:

"All dreams are valid"

VII

the vase shakes…
a dark tree sprouts out

on its top, seven tulips
close one after another

you touch—
each tumbles like a snowflake…

the snake creeps in…
the vase cracks
      …broken
         rib$
   you wake up

*   David Day, *The Animals Within*

** Margaret Atwood, *Another Visit to the Oracle*

父親的殿堂

當父親重建這座房子，
在每個梯階上，
他刻下他和母親的名字。
父親不是一個迷信或富有的人，
而我們都已長大，生活在很遠的城市，
他那高聳狹窄的四層建築
與我們對浪費不停息的批評一起挺立。
父親打破他的沉默，
「找到自己的樓層，待些日子吧。」
他眨著眼睛看著我們，
「至少無法出售。」

父親的智慧被城市規劃澈底擊敗。
工作人員帶來推土機，並要求他離開。
父親爬上屋頂，拒絕搬遷。
舉起相機，父親照下了他的最後一張
留念——在一群被推倒的拆遷房之中。

我收到一份當地報紙和照片的副本。
在廢墟上方，父親看著如此渺小。
標題很醒目：「最後的殿堂」。

My Father's Temple

When my father rebuilt his house,
on each stair he carved
his and my mother's names.
My father is not a superstitious or rich man,
with all of us grown up and living far away,
his narrow tall four-floor building
rose with our criticisms of its waste.
My father rolled his eyeballs, broke his silence:
"Find your own floor and stay longer."
He winked at us,
"At least none would buy."

My father's wisdom was defeated by the city plan.
Officers came along with bulldozers and demanded he leave.
My father climbed up to the roof, and refused to move.
Holding his camera, my father shot his last photo
among the knocked down neighborhood.

I received a copy of the photo in the local newspaper.
My father looked so small on the top of the ruins,
It was titled, "The Last Temple."

無從知曉

你問我是否瞭解你──
時至今日，我依然記得
那古老的河流，石頭：
像鳥兒振翅，
蘆葦遮掩著呢喃。

你的手捧托著於我手
一如萌開著的百合
在蘆葦蒼茫的河床。
細雨簾幕般低垂
群星怒放──直到黎明

現在或以後，
我佇立於自己的陰影，
傾聽它們墜落──
在寂靜中。

當時光帶走我，
回聲猶在重語──
追憶已是枉然。

Beyond My Knowing

You ask if I know you—
by now, I still remember
the old river, stones
slapped like birds.

Your hands cup mine
as a sprouting lily
among the white reed bed.
Curtain-like drizzle hangs
and stars till dawn.

Now and later,
I stand like a beacon,
listening to the stillness.

如何畫你？

「裸體」，我主張
「為了真相」。
你堅持抹去「臉部容顏」──
你把它留在中國古代，
月光下，
影子與焰火般荷花起舞。

遍歷你的年鑑，
褪色的里程碑，
分水嶺和生命線的穿插──
在內心深處，我看到了泰坦尼克號。

來，我把畫筆揮動──
你已經給了我所有的膽量：
紅色的河流，紅色的血脈，
紅色的沉默，紅色的頭蓋……
從畫框到畫框，
從天空到天空，
星星在慘澹的樹梢上綻放。

別處，硬幣覆蓋

你的眼睛，

在你的肌膚紋身上⋯⋯

我畫上一個異域風景。

注：「泰坦尼克號」台譯「鐵達尼號」。

How to Paint You?

"Naked", I claim, "for the sake of truth…"
"No facial view" you insist—
you have left it in ancient China,
under the moonlight,
shadows dancing with a flaming lotus.

Traversing your yearbook,
the faded milestones,
the shallow boundary by river banks
and the unmapped lifelines—
deep down, I see the Titanic.

Come, I wave a vast paintbrush—
you have given all your guts to me:
the red rivers, your red veins,
the red silence, your red hood…
from frame to frame,
from sky to sky,
stars loom upon bleak treetops.

Elsewhere, coins cover
your eyes,
tattoos on your skin…
I paint a foreign landscape.

How to Paint You?

夜行的列車

最後一次通話，
我們談到天氣，談到風景。
春天終於來了，
我開始原諒漫長的冬季，
並且刻意不提到——
那些寒冷的日子，詩來取暖。
我輕描淡寫另一個時區
紅梅也許開放。

我們都是孤兒。
記得18歲生日收到一本日記
如此精緻和美麗，
我寫下了手記，只為你保留。
然而，我的筆跡　沒有變得更好，
我的詩也沒能更成熟，
於是日記一直封裝著，最終丟失。

詩是繩索，為失落者放下來……
我們的通話以瑪麗.奧利弗的詩句結束。

窗外，火車來了又去。
我瞥見帶翅膀的影子，
那些羽毛只在夢中翱翔。

Late Trains

In our last call we talked about weather.

Spring is finally here and I forgave the long winter.

I intended not to mention those cold nights —

I moon-watered your poems.

They flowed into my veins, softening

my snow-buried garden…

No point to worry you,

I remarked that the wintersweet bloomed

…I could send you some shoots.

We two are orphans.

I remember a precious diary given to me

for my eighteenth birthday, so delicate and exquisite.

I wrote in it and saved it for you.

My handwriting still hasn't become better;

my best poems haven't arrived.

The diary grew out-of-date and eventually was lost.

Our call ended with Mary Oliver's line,

poems are ropes to let down for the lost…

Outside my window, night trains
come and go. I catch shadows
of wings that only soar in dreams.

作別向日葵

一百萬支箭對準天空，
也射不下太陽，
一轉眼的回眸，
金黃的臉盛滿淚水。
我的眼睛長滿憂鬱的草，
風中燎燎地燒。

那些浮萍，游魚，
那些雲影，輕風──
都留在身後
麥黃的熱浪中。

轉彎處我已迷途，
碎裂片片蓮心，
箭從手中穿過，
看得見落日的腥紅。

Farewell to Sunflowers

A million arrows are aimed at the sky,
yet the sun still is not shot down.
Glancing back,
their golden faces are soaked with tears.
Mourning grasses
grow wild upon my eyes,
burn flames in the wind.

Those duckweeds and swimming fish,
those floating clouds and breezes
are far behind.

In turning, I lose my way
and feel the lotus core in pieces.
With arrows sifting through my hand,
I see sunset in crimson.

告別交響曲

——聽海頓故事和他的同名交響曲有感

秋季的天空明朗淺藍，
蘆葦野曠裡高高地挺立。
而鳥聲漸弱，樹枝稀疏，
河流默然承接著葉落。

遠處的影子更深更長，
散碎的色調中，山川無聲無息。
深谷裡，風不斷地盤旋，
誰家的燭光還在遠遠召喚？

雪不久會覆蓋地面的一切，
大雁回望中開始飛行。
它們嘈雜的叫聲落下，
淹沒，退潮中一片蒼白。

The Farewell Symphony
—listening to Haydn

Another autumn sky, blue and clear,
out in wild fields reeds stretch.
Birdcalls fade in thin branches,
rivers silently gather fallen leaves.

Shadows grow dark and tall;
hills mute in shattered hues.
Winds spiral in deep valleys,
whose home, candles still beckon?

Soon snow will blanket everything below;
wild geese glance back and take off.
Their raucous echoes fall,
then drown, pale in ebbs.

內心的樹
——讀帕斯有感

我看到你
在玻璃裡面——
光線移動，
你也動了。

我走向你，
渴望將你拉出來。
一隻鳥向著你飛去，
崩一聲，她倒下。

我默念她。
黑夜降臨。
我想　我失去了你。你們兩個。

退回窗前，我打開燈，
你又出現，凝視著
我手裡的一枝羽毛。

我看見自己輕撫羽絲……
從上空我注視到河流，魚
和星一般的眼睛。

夜空加重了羽翼，
一棵樹形成；
我看得見形狀，顏色
和突然的降雨──

你家鄉的岩石上，
一棵松樹挺立，
在你必經的道路上
　一樹櫻花點亮……

我關掉燈，
內心的火焰閃動──
樹移動，
我也移動。

我們移動。

The Tree Within
—After reading Octavio Paz's A Tree Within

Here I see you
through the thin glass —
the light moves,
you move too.

I come toward you —
to pull you out.
A bird takes off…Bang!
She crashes.

I mourn for her.
The darkness descends.
I lose you.　　Both.

Bending down…
A feather lands on my palm;
I see waves, fish and starry eyes.

The night sky begins to grow
heavy feathers.
It draws a tree within…

I catch the shape, the sound
and sudden rains—where a pine tree
breaks through the rocky hill of your hometown—
where cherry blossoms rest
on the path you have come along…

I turn off the light—
the flames inside glow.
The tree moves,
I move too.

We move.

巒山之行

二十年後的今天，
你來信問詢，
記否巒山之行？

說那青翠的山林，
鬱鬱蔥蔥的心情；
說那鄉土的地鋪，
野曠天低的星雲。

光陰的流逝
刻在了久遠的記憶裡。
如今的山林
空落得映照自己的身影，
那溶洞還是深不可及，
只有風和著潮湧，
或明或滅的燭影裡，
你聽見足音飄遠……

沉沉的字句
抖不開夜的黑，
你說，
回味是重聚的黎明。

Trip to Lan Hill

After twenty years,
today I receive your letter
asking if I still remember
the trip to Lan Hill.

You mention the lush forest
the dense scent of pines.
Recall the campsite,
sparse and serene.

From the distant cave,
the dim flow of time
surges.
Shadows of an empty wood
tremble in candlelight.

Your words echo
first sunrays of dawn.

「晚安！」

再一次想起洋蔥，
我正啃一顆金色的蘋果。
褪了皮，我有點惋惜那光滑的纖質。
我的心臟需要一點暖色的補充，
持蘋果手機的人們互道著縹緲的問候。

哦，祝你健康快樂。重複著
卻無從定義，就像此刻
好想和你說一些笑話和往事，
卻總覺得像褪著洋蔥的外衣。

遙遠的街燈一盞盞熄滅，
這樓閣裡落寞的靜物畫
比我的果盤落寞。
新鮮如一的絢麗多了更深的
陰影，我渡過來渡過去
晚安，這樣簡單的語句。
而朝陽隱在某處，
片言隻語的沉默。

"Goodnight!"

Once again, I think of onions
while biting a golden apple.
Peeling its skin, I take pity on
its wasted smooth fibrous quality.
My heart needs warm supplement;
greetings from iPhones come and go,
yet all are ethereal tales.

Wish you health and happiness…
easily said but less weighty…
For this kind of lost moment, what I truly want
is to tell a few jokes and weep inside
like peeling another onion.

Distant street lamps, one by one,
blink off…
the solitary Still Life up high
is lonelier than a fruit plate.
Its gorgeous fresh color among deep
shadows, I pace back and forth—
Goodnight, such a simple statement.
Yet the sun is hidden somewhere,
utterances of silence.

聊天記錄

除了寒暄和謝謝，
更多的是互道晚安。
我的不安在於借用，
在於尋找某個出入口。
月亮永遠是個主題，
但那太遙遠，圍繞她的討論
超出了太陽星系
和一曲「一江水」的深度。

你說我是天使，我笑說不敢。
天使都是從天而降，
不像Google上隨意可以找到
電影天使，電腦病毒天使
和墮落天使⋯⋯
只是遺漏了「雪地天使」。
我有點遺憾。
這裡的冬天，我們習慣於自製——
只要平躺下來，四肢滑動。
當我們離開，天使們卻留了下來。

天亮了，我們聊天也將結束，
一個陌生人的博客上：
每一個女孩都曾經是一個無淚的天使。
當她遇見心愛的男孩時，便有了眼淚。

窗前的玫瑰凝著露珠，
我告訴你今天是個晴天。

WeChat

We greet, we thank,

and we say goodbye.

My anxiety about this shallow peace

struggles to find an entrance and an exit.

The moon seems a fond topic, of course,

but it is too aloof beyond this discussion.

We recall a song that sings

life and dreams are forever

on a river's opposite sides.

You sigh I am an angel; I fear not.

Angels are from heaven,

not the random results from Google,

too many and all kinds of:

Angelfish, Angels Trumpet, Angel Eyes,

Computer Virus Angels and Fallen Angels…

It is a pity that the search engine

has omitted the Snow Angel.

Winter is here, we get used to making many—

just lying down and sliding limbs,

when getting up, we leave angels behind.

The twilight breaks through,

we will soon end our chatting.

A post on a stranger's blog states:

"Every girl was once an angel without tears.

When she met her beloved, she began to taste tears."

The rose by my window sparkles with dew

I tell you today is sunny.

山水記

這時候，我們就像兩岸，
一本書，你翻看扉頁時，
我已越過後記。
打開關上再打開，
黑夜的天空，
流星如雨。
我把手遞給你，
憑欄處，應許之地，
我們低頭祈禱。
月光傾瀉下來，
海峽留下時光的顫慄。
多年以後，
有人捧在手上，
「錯過」如此鮮明。

Landscape Notes

Here and now, we are both

banks of a river.

The book, as you

read its title page,

I am reaching its appendix.

Open - close - open again,

the night sky,

meteor shower like rain.

I spread my hand to you,

beside the railing,

the Promised Land.

Bowing our heads we pray.

The moonlight pours down,

leaving the trembling waves on the strait.

Many years later,

someone will hold this in their hands:

"Mistake" is so eye-catching.

回家的地圖

圍繞地球儀，
你搜索著 兩個點，
由一條　飛行路線連接。
距離 成為一條長長的絲線
編織著濃濃的鄉愁；
你的手指輕推
藍色球體──故鄉
是掛在天上的一輪明月
傷痛地召喚。

兒子邀你繪製家譜樹。
你畫著一個個同心圓，
讓他很是詫異。
你的筆漂移，勾畫出
太陽星系的輪廓，
它們都圍繞同一點：
這就是我們的家園！

嬉笑你瘋狂的繪圖，
兒子裁剪延伸的家譜樹。
他沒有注意到
年輪漣漪著
夜色下的河流，
而葉子
落下
聚攏在根底。

The Map Home

Around the globe, you search
for two dots, connected
by a flight line. Distance
becomes a long string
to knot nostalgia;
Fingers nudge a blue
sphere – home beckons
like an aching moon.

Your son asks
to map the family tree.
You surprise him, draw
concentric circles. Your pen drifts,
traces solar systems,
that revolve around the same point—
That's our home!

Laughing at your crazy map,
your son prunes the growing tree.
He does not see
rings rippling across
your night river,
and leaves fall to roots.

回聲

親愛的，告訴我
你在這裡等我
告訴我，當墜入愛河時
甚至陰影
也有美麗的形式
告訴我，冬天並不冷
雪像棉花糖一樣甜美，
即使在睡夢時
有人陪我一起行走
告訴我，每隻鳥回到巢中
而光亮來自內心
告訴我，有很多可以夢想
並且期望
如此明亮，彷彿
無數的星星。
親愛的，告訴我，即使
保持沉默，你仍然可以
聽到我的聲音
並一次又一次地召喚
就像一面鏡子
我們面對面。

The Echo

Sweetheart, tell me
you are here for me
tell me when falling in love
even shadows
have beautiful forms
tell me winter is not cold
and snow tastes like sugar
tell me even in my sleep
someone walks with me
tell me each bird has a nest
and light is from inside
tell me plenty to dream of
and to hope…
so bright, as if
countless stars.
Sweetheart tell me even if
I am silent you still hear me
and call me again and again
so much like the mirror
we face each other.

當你老了
——讀葉芝偶感

當你老了，
某個冬夜，我會不期然來到。
在你靜寂的爐火前，
看著你緩緩地沉睡。
也許我會親吻一下你的額頭，
那裡犁田一樣耕耘著收穫，
也許我還會撫摸你蒼老的手掌，
讀著你未盡的心事。

爐火會慢慢褪去，
飛揚的雪總會抹去我來去的痕跡，
也許你已經忘記，
在你的夢裡重現的青春
烙印的詩句，
在月光下
被一個人靜靜憶起。

When You Are Old

—*After Yeats*

When you are old,

I may arrive at night.

Without your expecting,

sitting by a quiet fire,

I will watch you sleep.

I may kiss your forehead

where time plows deep wisdom.

I may caress your rough palm

and soothe your incomplete wishes.

The fire will slowly die out.

Falling snow will cover my footprints.

And you, you may forget

the recurring youth of your dreams

and your poems in print,

recalled by someone

who wanders under the moon.

* 攝影｜岑賢道

鳴謝｜Special Thanks

　　二十年，彈指一揮間。回望中有眼淚也有歡笑，更多的是光亮，透過樹林和書行，帶給我欣喜寬慰，也安放我心，久久難忘。猶如燈塔之光，引領我內心的那個孩子在繁雜的人世間和海外生活的交融中找到心之歸屬，也聚成一本本詩集。

　　這裡我要衷心感謝多年來東西方媒體和詩刊的厚愛，感謝中英文詩歌評委和詩友的肯定，感謝加拿大出版社「Mosaic Press」和「Black Moss Press」相繼出版我的英文詩集，並向高等學府和詩歌獎推薦。是詩路上相遇的知己同行以及家人親友的支持鼓勵，讓我在異域生活中以詩人和電腦工程師的雙重身分，用兩種語言豐富自己，廣拓視野，勤於創作，詩意人生。

　　我更要感謝辛牧老師向秀威資訊推薦《愛的燈塔》，惠謝出版社鄭伊庭主任和陳慈蓉編輯以及團隊的悉心設計和編輯排版，以讓台灣以及更多的海外讀者遇見我，因詩結緣，彼此點亮。前行路上，無論歲月流轉，青春不再，但心裡永結夢想和童心。愛的燈塔不會熄滅，夢的旅程不會終結，就像我即將啟程的羅馬之行，去到那永恆之城，那名字寫在水裡的，會永記在這一片光亮裡。

　　　　　　　　　　　　星子安娜（2019/06/16）於多倫多

出版說明｜Notes

　　本書部分詩作曾獲以下中英文刊物及詩選的肯定，衷心感謝各位主編以及評委：

　　《創世紀詩雜誌》《中國日報》《詩天空》《北美楓》《新大陸詩刊》《四海為詩：旅美華人離散詩精選》《世界日報》《北美時報》《新文學》《常青藤詩刊》《綠色生活》《華人時刊》《眾筆匯華章》《世界華文作家》《騰上行》……

　　CBC Radio, *Arc Poetry, Literary Review of Canada, Canadian Immigrant Magazine, Windsor Review, The Toronto Quarterly, Cha: An Asian Literary Journal, Women's Voices for Change, A Canadian Anthology of Poetry 2018 etc.*

獲獎詩作 | Poems that won awards

2005: "Toronto, No More Weeping" won Ted Plantos Memorial Award from The Ontario Poetry Society

2008: "The Woman within Her House" won the second place for 12th Mattia Family International Poetry Contest

2009: "Raspberries" was nominated by Cha: An Asian Literary Journal for Pushcart Prize

2010: "After reading Ted Hughes' 'Full Moon and Little Frieda'" won the Poem-A-Day contest in Cambridge, Ontario

2015: "The Sin City" won Honorable Mention Awards in the Open Heart 9 Poetry Contest by Ontario Poetry Society

出版作品 | Publications

　　《Wings Toward Sunlight》由加拿大擁有40多年歷史的Mosaic Press出版，以其清新簡約的印象派詩畫特色以及東方意境和深刻內涵引起廣泛注意和好評。Reid Mitchell稱安娜簡約溫婉以及疊句技巧讓他想起中國宋代女詞人李清照，Elana Wolff則稱她讀到了美國獲獎詩人Mary Oliver的樸素和獨特的意象與自然的融合。詩歌評委John.B.Lee認為安娜心裡住著東西方詩人，在她的詩作裡，既可看到李白於月共舞，又可感覺到Emily Dickinson 燈下沉思。

Wings Toward Sunlight，2011 出版。

　　兩年後同家出版社對安娜的詩歌在構思和內容上趨向更廣泛的社會問題和人文思想給予肯定，繼續出版她的英文詩集《Inhaling the Silence》。詩集第一部分「夜歌」以抒情為主，優美流暢，熱烈深沉，既根植於中國傳統的景觀和文化，也借鑒穿插著北美文化。第二部分「藍色星球上」，以嚴謹樸實的詩風展示現實與環境，經濟和社會等矛盾。Richard Greene 稱安娜的作品更

Inhaling the Silence，2013 出版。

成熟更奇妙,把看似不相關的意象巧妙地放在一起,讀後讓人深思回味。Terry Barker稱安娜的詩理性又率性,既矛盾又內在統一,也許正是安娜所認識的這個世界,光亮和黑暗共存,希望與失望同在。

　　2015年加拿大另一家歷史悠久的出版社Black Moss Press出版了安娜的《Seven Nights with the Chinese Zodiac》。書名同題詩為一組七首象徵意味的短詩,借鑒了中國十二生肖,《動物農場》以及聖經故事。加拿大國家桂冠詩人George Elliott Clarke稱讚這是安娜在夢境和現實中相互參照,將東西方文化藝術和神話延伸的浪漫虛幻結合,也是值得借鑒反思的作品集。Doyali Islam評論這本詩集不僅是關於時間的不可阻擋的流逝,以及對個人和社會文明的意義,也是對所有生命的慶祝,就像螢火蟲在她的《生命瓶罐》中一樣奇妙——只要我們停下來傾聽和閱讀。

　　《Nightlights》是以日本俳句方式的系列英文短詩集。在這裡安娜找到自己與自然最簡單最樸實的親近方

Seven Nights with the Chinese Zodiac,2015出版。

Nightlights,2017出版。

式，在片刻和生活的細微處發現美和真實。從現代生活的緊張節奏中，她更希望人們慢下來去感受生活，感受自然，而不是旅程的過客，匆匆路人。因此在加拿大安大略省，她開發了系列藝術專案，並在擔任第一屆密西沙加桂冠詩人的兩年間發起詩歌推廣活動。而這本詩集和詩歌短片及時地充當了深入淺出的教材，引導人們打開心扉，感受自然和生活的美好時刻。

語言文學類　PG2309　秀詩人64

愛的燈塔
——星子安娜雙語詩選

作　　者/Anna Yin（星子安娜）
責任編輯/陳慈蓉
圖文排版/莊皓云
封面設計/楊廣榕

發　行　人/宋政坤
法律顧問/毛國樑　律師
出版發行/秀威資訊科技股份有限公司
　　　　　114台北市內湖區瑞光路76巷65號1樓
　　　　　電話：+886-2-2796-3638　傳真：+886-2-2796-1377
　　　　　http://www.showwe.com.tw
劃撥帳號/19563868　戶名：秀威資訊科技股份有限公司
　　　　　讀者服務信箱：service@showwe.com.tw
展售門市/國家書店（松江門市）
　　　　　104台北市中山區松江路209號1樓
　　　　　電話：+886-2-2518-0207　傳真：+886-2-2518-0778
網路訂購/秀威網路書店：https://store.showwe.tw
　　　　　國家網路書店：https://www.govbooks.com.tw

2019年9月　BOD一版
定價：290元
版權所有　翻印必究
本書如有缺頁、破損或裝訂錯誤，請寄回更換

國家圖書館出版品預行編目

愛的燈塔：星子安娜雙語詩選 / Anna Yin著. -- 一版. --
臺北市：秀威資訊科技, 2019.09
　　面；　公分. -- (語言文學類；PG2309)(秀詩人；64)
中英對照
BOD版
ISBN 978-986-326-729-4(平裝)

874.51   108013139

讀者回函卡

感謝您購買本書，為提升服務品質，請填妥以下資料，將讀者回函卡直接寄回或傳真本公司，收到您的寶貴意見後，我們會收藏記錄及檢討，謝謝！如您需要了解本公司最新出版書目、購書優惠或企劃活動，歡迎您上網查詢或下載相關資料：http:// www.showwe.com.tw

您購買的書名：_____

出生日期：_____年_____月_____日

學歷：□高中 (含) 以下　　□大專　　□研究所 (含) 以上

職業：□製造業　□金融業　□資訊業　□軍警　□傳播業　□自由業
　　　□服務業　□公務員　□教職　　□學生　□家管　　□其它_____

購書地點：□網路書店　□實體書店　□書展　□郵購　□贈閱　□其他

您從何得知本書的消息？

　□網路書店　□實體書店　□網路搜尋　□電子報　□書訊　□雜誌
　□傳播媒體　□親友推薦　□網站推薦　□部落格　□其他_____

您對本書的評價：(請填代號　1.非常滿意　2.滿意　3.尚可　4.再改進)

　封面設計____　版面編排____　內容____　文／譯筆____　價格____

讀完書後您覺得：

　□很有收穫　□有收穫　□收穫不多　□沒收穫

對我們的建議：_____

_____

_____

_____

11466
台北市內湖區瑞光路 76 巷 65 號 1 樓

秀威資訊科技股份有限公司　　　收

BOD 數位出版事業部

⋯⋯⋯⋯⋯⋯⋯⋯⋯⋯⋯⋯⋯⋯⋯⋯⋯⋯⋯⋯⋯⋯⋯⋯⋯⋯⋯⋯⋯⋯⋯

（請沿線對折寄回，謝謝！）

姓　　名：＿＿＿＿＿＿＿＿＿　年齡：＿＿＿＿　性別：□女　□男

郵遞區號：□□□□□

地　　址：＿＿＿＿＿＿＿＿＿＿＿＿＿＿＿＿＿＿＿＿＿＿＿＿＿

聯絡電話：(日) ＿＿＿＿＿＿＿＿＿＿＿ (夜) ＿＿＿＿＿＿＿＿＿＿

E-mail：＿＿＿＿＿＿＿＿＿＿＿＿＿＿＿＿＿＿＿＿＿＿＿＿＿